DO YOU LOVE ME?

*A romantic journey of
self-discovery and acceptance.*

*As a newborn, she was abandoned and
thrown in an alley dumpster. As a prominent
doctor, will she find the mystery behind her
birth?*

By
Millie Pérez

Do You Love Me?
A romantic journey of self-discovery and acceptance.
by Millie Pérez

Printed in the United States of America

ISBN 9781628391961

www.xulonpress.com

Table of Contents

Dedication

I would like to dedicate this book to my children, David and Isaac Gonzalez. They make me a better person, inspire me to reach for the stars and fill my life with adventure.

To my husband Oscar Gonzalez, for his unceasing encouragement, love, support and his downright PUSHING! LOL. Thank you sweetie for believing in me!

To my mother, for sacrificing so much to instill in me the principles that I now pass down to my children. Mom, your pain was my gain; it brought about life for generations. Thank you!

To my sisters Sandra, Marta & Sonia thank you for putting up with my madness for so many years; it's finally paying off. I can write about it instead of making you crazy with it! LOL

To my nieces and nephews Yairy, Melissa, Stephanie, Gam, Omar, Leo, Yarissa; who created in me a love for children that I never knew I could have. You were my first love and now you are my encouragers and fans.

To my awesome friends — you know who you are — for believing in me, supporting me and competing to be my number one fan. LOL

Last but not least, to my FGAL readers. It was because of your support and feedback that I was able to gain enough courage to submit this novel for publishing. I love you all so much! Yaaaaay!! We did it!!! www.fourgirlsandalady.blogspot.com

Introduction

*J*ust to give you a little background, I have always been an avid reader. My favorite books to read are biographies, novels and self-help books. However, I never thought I would be writing one of my own one day. It wasn't until this year 2013, when my husband encouraged me to start a blog that I realized I truly enjoyed writing.

My blog, "Four Girls And a Lady" was where my love of writing began. It was on that blog that I began sharing my life experiences, my mother's struggles as a single mom raising four girls, the hardship of her divorce, my childhood lessons, and so on. After a few months, I began to share my opinions about relationships, raising children, traveling, and much more. After only four months my blog had received over 20,000 hits. I was amazed, it was completely unexpected.

On one occasion I decided to look at the blog stats and realized I had readers with ages ranging from thirteen to sixty three; men and woman from all over the world. The blog was being visited daily from over ten countries. That was truly exciting and motivating. I saw it as an opportunity to influence the young ones and learn from the mature ones.

With a feeling of great responsibility I began to brainstorm about creative ways I could mentor the young ones, while at the same time have something for every age group to enjoy. That's when the idea of a novel came to mind. I thought, if I could capture their attention through fiction, it would be a great way to provide scenarios for life lessons for all generations.

In this novel, you will notice that there is a life lesson for every age group. In the beginning, you will be taken on a woman's journey from mother to grandmother. From her, you will learn the value of the little things and the importance of living intentionally. You will then be taken through the life journey of another woman, from whom you will learn where the source of respect, admiration and love springs from.

In closing, I truly enjoyed writing **Do You Love Me?** I fell in love with the characters, the setting and just about everything. I pray that I will have the opportunity to write many more. Thanks for reading!

What people are saying about Do You Love Me?

As I started to read this novel it literally, captivated my full attention. After reading the first few paragraphs of the story, sooner than later I began indulging in it; I'm so very glad I did. This story is amazing! I haven't read a novel like this in years. It really touched me and even had me in tears a little. I was amazed at the suspense it had me in. I'm now a fan of her novels. I guess I will read them for my own entertainment throughout my travels. In my opinion, Millie has emerged to her true self through the gift of writing. I enjoyed this novel immensely and would recommend it to all of my friends. There is a message of hope and great inspiration to everybody that reads this story and the ones to come, I'm sure. Great job Millie Perez!

Roberto Hernandez
Inspirational speaker and life coach.
www.thepurposeman.com

I want to praise the author, Millie Perez. Only a person with life experiences of her own can "tap" into the depths of the emotion of her readers. Every word was placed perfectly together as a harmony synchronized with a perfect melody. My dear friend Millie, may the pen of your heart never stop writing.

Lizzett Alvarado
Singer, songwriter and conference speaker.

*I was immediately captivated by the story of Abigail in **Do You Love Me?** The story of Abigail made me laugh, cry, and even think about my own insecurities. Millie, your writing is a gift that can only be described as **God-given**. If this is a short novel, and the beginning of your storytelling; I am eagerly awaiting your first book. Thank you for allowing me to review your work. I am humbled to have even been considered. You are an inspiration for me to begin working on my own dream. Please continue to bless us with your beautiful story telling.*

Karitsa Mills
Graduate of Ryder University and school teacher.

CHAPTER 1

Pulled From A Dumpster

She was born on a snowy winter night. Snow-flakes covered the town like a glistening blanket. Bare, lifeless trees took on an enchanting look. Every branch was perfectly decorated with sparkling snow. The light of the full moon illuminated the town; the snow made the town seem magical with an indescribable glow.

She was beautifully made, with lush brown hair that covered her perfectly rounded head, her olive skin matched her perfect brown eyes, and her tiny apple-red lips appeared to be smiling. The doctor held the helpless baby and questioned, "Who could have left this baby in a street dumpster?" It would seem unimaginable if it hadn't been for the countless times she'd seen similar things. Even still, there was no getting used to the pain it caused her. She'd seen firsthand how these children got lost in the system and ended up with less-than-perfect futures. Sometimes she really hated her job. After so many years of being a doctor, one would have thought she'd gotten used to seeing tragedy, but seeing kids suffer always did this to her. She looked at the scrapes on the baby's little legs, caused by the trash that surrounded her when thrown into the dumpster. She had to let her go, she passed the baby on to Nurse Sal Lopez to be cleaned. On she went to her next patient.

The baby was found by a student nurse one block away from the Metropolitan Hospital. He told the police that as he walked to the hospital's parking garage he heard a baby crying. He followed the tiny voice and found himself in the alley behind the garage. The crying was coming from a dumpster. He ran towards it and using crates to prop himself up, he looked inside and saw the baby. He described her as naked, bloody, and with the umbilical cord still attached. He called 911 and climbed over to pick up the child. Within minutes the paramedics arrived, they attached a small ladder to the dumpster. The student nurse handed the baby to them, and immediately the baby was taken to Metropolitan hospital's ER where Dr. Lourdes attended her.

Dr. Lourdes was a woman in her mid forties with three kids of her own, Richard Jr., Emily and Isaac. Her husband Richard Sr. was slightly older than her and a prominent minister. As far back as she could remember she knew she wanted to be a doctor. While her friends were dressing up their dolls for strolls around the park, Lourdes was undressing hers to give them an examination. She loved the thought of making someone feel better and taking part in helping them. Lourdes's mother often told friends of a time when she was five years old. She set up the driveway to resemble a waiting room and used paint cans as seats. She asked three of her friends to sit and wait for their turn to get their check-up. The garage was set up with a small table where her friends had to sit to be examined. The funny thing about the story was the sickness she chose for each child: one had an "ear" headache, the other a "chest" stomachache, and the last kid, who was the only boy, had pink eye. The girls, of course, took care of making the area under his eyes appear irritated by using pink markers. Although she got in trouble for painting the kid's face, her mother admitted she admired her creativity and her passion to help others even in pretend games.

While driving home from work that night, all Lourdes could think about was that baby. She wondered who could have done such a terrible thing. It was cold and snowy; that baby could have easily died. Why did she make it? What awaited her? She was surprised by her emotional reaction that day when the nurses were picking the baby's name. She usually stayed away from that process. She was not good at showing emotion in front of her nurses, or in front of anyone for that matter. However, as she heard them throw names around, she could not help herself...out of nowhere, she said, "Her name will be Abigail."

It was two o'clock in the morning by the time Lourdes arrived at her house; she sat in her car, admiring it for a few minutes. It was the house of her dreams. She remembered as a teenager drawing a house almost exactly like the one she owned, minus the Olympic-sized pool, bowling alley and miniature golf course. She smiled at the thought. It was breathtaking, if she said so herself. The Victorian custom-built home sat on a hillside. It was painted in a serene, soft yellow tone with chalk white shutters to accent the French windows. Her favorite part of the house was the wraparound porch. All four front windows were decorated with wicker baskets, where she had colorful tulips planted every spring; even though now they looked more like ice buckets.

She sighed as she got out of the car and headed towards the front door. Once inside, she walked around the house quietly trying not to wake anyone. She entered each one of her children's rooms and kissed them on the head. There had been a sense of guilt inside of her since she had her first child that never let go. Lourdes worked long days and many nights. She wondered if true balance could ever be achieved. She couldn't help but feel that her children were getting the short end of the stick when it came to their mom. Just for one day Lourdes would like to feel free of guilt, sadness, and frustration. She couldn't remember the last time she felt joy.

Lourdes was awakened by the warm, gentle rays of the sun. She loved it when the sun kissed her good morning. She hurried to the kitchen to make the family breakfast before they headed out to school. She enjoyed being at home to see the kids off. One by one, they woke up as they smelled the aromas of a hearty breakfast: scrambled eggs, bacon, pancakes, coffee and a bowl of oatmeal. Everyone's favorite was covered. The family sat at the table for a quick ten minutes; Lourdes wished she could freeze time.

There was so much to say, to ask, to share, but there was never enough time. Everyone went their separate ways and she was left alone; just as her heart felt, alone.

As she prepared herself for work, she noticed something felt different. She couldn't wait to get to work. She hadn't felt like that in years, she couldn't understand it. The reason she had chosen to be an ER doctor was so that she wouldn't become attached to the patients. So why did she wake up thinking about baby Abigail? She tried to think about other things as she drove to the hospital. She turned on some music and sang along. But before she realized it, she found herself on the fifth floor; the hospital nursery. She looked desperately through the glass, but she didn't see the baby. She went inside and searched crib by crib, but there was no sign of her. She walked out, and there, in a corner of the corridor was a tiny crib with a pink ribbon. She rushed to it, upset at the thought that someone had left a baby unattended. When she got to it, the crib was empty. Puzzled, she looked on the side of the basin to see the name insert. It read "Abigail." In a panic she thought, *where did she go, who took her, will I ever see her again?* All these thoughts kept running across her mind, but why? Why did she care? What was wrong with her? Without a second thought, she slipped Abigail's name tag into her pocket.

Lourdes was angry with herself for her lack of professionalism. She would never ask anyone about that baby. Deep inside she knew if she found out where she was, she'd want to pursue her, care for her, keep her in her life. But she knew she didn't have time for that. She would just have to live without knowing; it was better that way. Why not? She had been able to do that all of her life with many things. She had deprived herself time after time of life's pleasures for the sake of what's best for others; this time would not be any different. Besides, getting attached to any patient, including a baby, would be nothing but unprofessional. She would never allow that from her staff, much less from herself. She attended patient by patient by patient but she was unable to finish her shift. Although by now she could work her shift almost blindfolded; she felt unsettled. Something was bothering her, she went home early.

On the drive home she tried to figure out what was going on with her. She thought about how great her life was: good kids, a husband who loved her, and a successful career. What more could she ask for? She felt ungrateful, even with the thought of perhaps wanting more. Lourdes was at a stoplight when she thought she saw a man carrying a baby wrapped in a pink blanket from the hospital. She got this strange feeling in her stomach. She felt as though she had to follow him. What if that was Abigail? She followed behind him with her car, acting as if she was lost and looking for an address. At that very moment, her phone rang. She was startled by the sound and afraid the man heard it too. She ducked behind the steering wheel, scrambled through her purse until she found her phone and answered it. As she made a list of things her kids needed her to stop and buy, she lost the man; he was nowhere to be found.

Three months passed since baby Abigail was born. Lourdes continued to think about her every day. She was glad the dark and gloomy days of winter had passed. She hoped the spring would help get her spirits up. She wasn't a fan of the dark days of winter. She spent the last three months in sort of a daze. Every day after work, she would drive around the area where she had seen the man with the baby, hoping she would one day see them again. It was strange how even though she didn't get a good look at him, he somehow seemed familiar. She laughed at the silliness of that thought. Deep down, she knew the odds of that were slim. She had to move past this, but she couldn't. Her days were filled with regrets and sadness. Days turned to weeks, weeks to months and months to five years.

CHAPTER 2

Will I Ever See Her Again?

*E*very year Lourdes hosted a staff appreciation BBQ at her house. This was the first time that she decided to encourage everyone to bring their families and pets to meet one another and share. She thought it would be a good idea to create a sense of family within the staff. The sweet smell of flowers in bloom and the fresh, crisp winds of spring filled the air. Spring gave the hope of all things new, nature came back to life and color took over the fields. Lourdes's rose garden was in full bloom: red, white, yellow, and pink roses surrounded her front yard. Everything looked perfect, round tables were dressed with delicate colorful flowered print tablecloths, and glass vases filled with flowers from her garden graced the center of each table.

As the staff arrived, Lourdes and her family welcomed them. She felt ashamed that most of the staff had worked many years for her, yet she didn't even know if some of them were married, let alone had children. A separate area had been prepared for the children; it was decorated lively and inviting. One of the first to arrive was Teresa with her three granddaughters; she was an older nurse who refused to retire. Lourdes couldn't understand why she was still working. She had caught her more than once sleeping on the job. One time, Teresa went so far as to pretend to be a patient so she could sleep through the night comfortably in one of the empty rooms. Lourdes couldn't help but laugh out loud at the thought of that one. Teresa was a good and efficient nurse; Lourdes would never get her in trouble for that. She did however, convince her to take the day shift.

Two families arrived at the same time, the Lopez's and the Patel's. They were her only two male nurses in the ER. She knew they were both married, but didn't know Mr. Lopez had children, four of them to be exact; two boys and two girls. Mr. Patel had two, a boy and a girl. Immediately following them, three more cars pulled up. They were the last of her guests, Nurse Jacquelyn, Nurse Jeannette and Nurse Evet. Altogether, they brought four kids. Evet wasn't married and didn't have any children, she brought her dog Yukon. She loved to travel, so she dedicated most of her life to exploring the world. Lourdes only knew this because of what she would hear them talk about in the nurses' lounge. The nurses were always trying to play matchmaker with Evet. They wanted every new young doctor to take her out on a date; it was pretty amusing.

The BBQ was in full swing with music, dancing and lots of eating. Everyone was having a great time getting to know each other's family. Every year everyone ended up gravitating to wherever Nurse Sal Lopez was. He'd been her head nurse for as long as she could remember. In some ways, Lourdes thought he was as close to a relative as she would allow an employee to be. He attended all her family functions; yet she didn't even know he had children. Mr. Patel was his partner in crime; together they would play jokes on the nurses. This year was no different. There they were, all the families gathered around them. Nurse Lopez appeared to be telling the families a story of some sort.

He was telling the families about one Halloween night when he and Patel arranged a practical joke to scare the girls. Nurse Patel played the patient (he was supposed to be off that night) and Nurse Lopez, the nurse in charge of him. In the middle of the night, Lopez called the other three nurses into the nurse's lounge and told them that he needed their opinion on his new patient. He said the patient had just been transferred from another hospital because they couldn't figure out what was wrong. He explained that the patient didn't speak, move, or opened his eyes, but that there appeared not to be anything medically wrong with him. He then leaned in and spoke softly when he told them that a nurse from the other hospital said she thought he was possessed. Nurse Lopez continued by telling them that the patient might end up in the psychiatric ward the next day, but that he wanted the girls to see him. He told them that the way the patient looked was the strangest thing of all — he didn't even look human. At that point, the girls were practically running to see the patient; curiosity was killing them. Nurse Lopez had strategically placed the "patient" (Nurse Patel) in a vacant side of the unit, a room far away enough from anyone else, so that no one would hear what was going on. The girls entered the room cautiously. The "patient" had the sheets over his face. Nurse Lopez was dramatic when removing the sheets… slowly, carefully, quietly. The nurses' eyes were practically popping out of their heads, they could hardly wait. Then all of the sudden, Nurse Patel let out an agonizing scream and attempted to grab the three girls. They started screaming and running down the hall. Patel ran after them, trying to stop them. Even after seeing Patel and Lopez laughing, they were so afraid that they continued running and screaming.

When Nurse Sal Lopez was done telling the story, the families laughed so loud that Lourdes wondered what they were talking about. She never took part in any chitchat with her staff; it seemed unprofessional. She wished she could. In that moment, she looked over to the children. Immediately she felt that all-too-familiar feeling she always felt when she heard or saw children. Some of those children were the age that Abigail would have been by now. She felt her stomach sink. Even after five years, she still thought of her every day. Sadness filled her soul, and she felt as though she was going to lose her composure. Two of the little girls came running towards her and gave her some flowers.

Lourdes could not contain herself any longer, she began to cry. Tears fell like a waterfall down her cheeks, tears she had been holding back for years. The girls were startled. One of them told her she was sorry and that she'd glue the flowers back in her garden. Lourdes couldn't answer. She ran inside the house and locked herself in her room. For the first time, she allowed herself to cry over Abigail. She sobbed uncontrollably, her body shook forcefully with the power of her emotional state. "WHY?" she yelled. "Why can't I find her?"

CHAPTER 3

A Good Life Isn't Good Enough

ourdes's longing to see Abigail continued throughout her life. After thirty years, she'd lost all hope of ever seeing her again.

Lourdes lived what most would consider a full life. At the end of her life, she found herself fighting a losing battle with lung cancer. Her daughter made sure she was surrounded by her favorite things. On both sides of her hospital bed, the nightstands held glass vases with roses of every color. Their fragrance filled the room with a sweet aroma. The bed was dressed with yellow sheets, her favorite color. Yellow reminded her of the warmth and brightness of the sun on a spring morning. She was wearing her favorite nightgown, soft cotton with a flowered print in all shades of yellow.

On the wall to her left, there were family pictures. First was her daughter Emily's wedding. She looked beautiful in her mother's wedding dress; what an honor that was for Lourdes. Having inherited her mother's taste, her wedding colors were yellow and white and her flowers were roses. Lourdes was glad her daughter had chosen her backyard for her wedding. Every time she sat on her back porch, she would reminisce about that special day.

Next to that picture was the picture of her oldest son Richard jr.'s graduation from graduate school. He received a master's degree in social work. She remembered that day as if it were yesterday. When her son's name was called to receive his diploma, he grabbed her by the hand and had her walk with him. It was his way of thanking her for all of the years she helped him with papers, projects, money and anything else he needed. He received a standing ovation from the audience for that. His mother, on the other hand, felt embarrassed and didn't like the attention.

Next was the picture of her youngest son Isaac's wedding. He was such a goof ball, always the life of the party. She was so proud of him. He had become a doctor and shared her love for medicine.

On the wall facing her bed was her fiftieth wedding anniversary picture. She could hardly believe how fast the time had passed. Her three kids had sneaked around for months to put together a surprise anniversary party for them. The wall on her right side had the pictures of her six grandchildren.

She was appreciative that the hospital allowed her daughter to decorate her room this way. They wanted to make her feel as comfortable as possible since she would not be leaving there; not alive anyway. That was the hospital's way of showing her some gratitude for all her years of service. Although she had been retired for quite some time, she was invited often to speak to the interns.

Lourdes looked around her room, she didn't know why she felt a void. She'd done everything right: lived by the rules, gave to charity, helped people in need, assisted church services and was a good mother and wife. Yet she still felt empty. All of her life she lived with the feeling that something was missing. She opened her hand and looked at the name tag she had taken from Abigail's nursery crib. She kept it in her purse and carried it around every where she went. At that moment she understood that what she was missing was Abigail. She held the name tag tightly as tears began to roll down the sides of her face.

Lourdes looked out the big window towards the sky; it looked like snow was coming. She could tell because the sky had a pinkish tone to it. The trees were bare and lifeless, the grass pale and dry. Winter–all things old–all things dead. Sadly, she knew enough about the disease to know that she only had days to live, perhaps hours. Her thoughts were interrupted by a doctor walking into her room to monitor her and ask how she was feeling. Although Lourdes couldn't speak, she motioned with her head and tried to communicate with her eyes. She blinked as if to say, "I'm as well as I could be." The doctor looked around the room, then looked at Lourdes. Dr. Lourdes knew she looked fragile, weak, and deteriorated; not at all like the woman who used to run around the hospital focused and determined. She could see from the expression on the Doctor's face that she was being looked at with pity; she knew that look all too well. She closed her eyes in anguish, hating to be looked upon like that. *Who was this doctor anyway?* She thought, surely it wasn't anyone Lourdes had seen before. She struggled to look at the badge. The doctor noticed and leaned in to show her.

"I'm Dr. Lopez, I know you don't know me personally, but I know you very well. I'm Nurse Sal Lopez's adopted daughter." Lourdes took a closer look at the doctor, analyzing every feature in her face. She noticed her lush brown hair, olive skin, beautiful brown eyes and apple red lips. She felt her heart racing and her breathing grew shallow and rapid, she desperately longed to be able to speak. *No, not on my death bed, not now!*

Dr. Lopez continued to speak, attempting to calm Lourdes. "I've accompanied my father to all the major events in your life." Dr. Lopez pointed to the pictures on the wall as she spoke. "I was there and there and there. We are members of your church and I did my internship under your team." Lourdes's eyes began to swell up with tears; her heart could hardly contain the emotion. The doctor sat on the edge of the bed and continued to speak. "I don't think you recognize me Dr. Lourdes, but that's okay, we have never formally talked. I admire women doctors, there aren't many of us. I wanted to be a doctor ever since my dad told me a woman doctor gave me my name. He never told me who. I hope I could meet her someday."

As Dr. Lopez spoke, she lovingly wiped the tears from Lourdes's face and gently stroked her hair. Lourdes wished she had not been such a hard woman to get to know. She wished she would have let her guard down long enough to notice. Tears she could no longer contain rolled down the sides of her face. She wanted to yell to the top of her lungs, "IT WAS ME, I named you! I searched for you all of my life. I looked for you everywhere; I never stopped looking. I can't believe you were there all along. In my house, my church, my job, how could this be! How could I have missed it? This just can't be happening. Why didn't I recognize you, why didn't I pay more attention? You were what I was looking for, what I needed, and you were there, but I missed it."

As she wept, she could not stop staring at Dr. Lopez's badge. She didn't want to believe the truth that was in front of her. *Could this really be her?*

"Is it my name Lourdes?" Dr. Lopez asked. Obviously clueless of the true reason behind Dr. Lourdes's agitation, she tried to calm her down by making small talk. "Oh I'm sorry, I never told you my first name did I? It's Abigail."

Lourdes opened her eyes wide. She could not stop herself from sobbing; there was no denying that it was Abigail, who was sitting on her bed. Lourdes's body was shaking with emotion. She took a deep breath while putting Abigail's hand in hers. Taking her last breath, she struggled to get some words out. Abigail was trying to calm her down; she knew Lourdes didn't have enough oxygen to speak. But she was desperately trying to say something. Gasping for air, she managed to whisper, "I know your name is Abigail, I named you; It means JOY."

The heart monitor flat lined. Dr. Lopez was doing everything in her power to keep her alive, but to no avail. She screamed, "No Dr. Lourdes, stay with me, please stay with me!!!" But Lourdes had gone into cardiac arrest and passed on. Abigail, ignoring all hospital ethics laid her head on her chest and cried. She was filled with emotion, she wasn't sure if what she heard was real. *Did I hear her right, did I hear her say she was the doctor that named me? Now I'll never know.* She was still holding Lourdes's hand when she felt that there was something in it. She took a closer look, it was an old shriveled up card of some sort. She opened it. It was a hospital baby's crib name tag; it had the name Abigail and her date of birth written on it. Abigail looked at Lourdes's lifeless body and began to sob "It was you? You named me Abigail? Why didn't you tell me sooner? I have so many questions!!!"

CHAPTER 4

Death Brings About A "prince"

The weather embodied the sadness of the event. The sky was covered in dark storm clouds. Deafening, rumbling thunder filled the air, while blazing lightning illuminated the sky. Four black cars carried hurting people; it was the day of Lourdes's burial. In a single file, her loved ones walked towards the grave site. Lourdes's husband Richard Sr., her children, Richard Jr., Emily and Isaac, along with her grandchildren, all sat in the first row of chairs under the purple canopy. The four rows of chairs behind them held her ex-coworkers and her friends. In a single chair at the very back of the canopy sat a woman dressed in a long-sleeve, high-collared, black dress. She was wearing a hat with a net attached, the net helped hide the anguish in her face. That woman was Dr. Abigail Lopez.

Sitting across from Abigail at the cemetery, was a section reserved for the prominent Metropolitan Hospital staff. Everyone was represented from the CEOs, chiefs of surgery, chiefs of medicine, and some head physicians. Just taking a glance their way made everyone feel like tiny worms. Most of them carried themselves with overbearing arrogance.

Abigail sat staring at Lourdes's family mourn; she felt selfish for incubating feelings of anger and frustration. In her mind, Abigail replayed over and over the last moments of Lourdes's life. There she laid, powerless and unable to speak. Indeed, she had a story to tell, Abigail could see it in the desperation in her face and the urgency she expressed through her body language. But Abigail had no idea that what Lourdes was so desperately trying to convey was her very own birth story.

Lourdes died knowing the mystery behind Abigail's birth. It was a mystery because it was something Abigail had been trying to discover her entire adult life. Lourdes knew what happened; she held the key that could have answered all of her questions. Although Abigail had never shared that with anyone, there were questions that circled around in her head like a merry-go-round each and every day. She wondered about the circumstances behind her adoption; were her parents forced to give her up because they were too young? Did her mother cry as she handed her over to strangers? Was she purchased from an adoption agency? How much was her life worth when or if she was purchased? The more she thought about it, the more she had to fight to hold back her tears.

Her parents always changed the subject when she asked about how she had been adopted. Her father would tell her it wasn't important, and her adoptive mother just didn't want to be bothered.

She looked up to see the minister staring right at her as he said, "Let us learn from the way Lourdes lived her life. She accomplished all that she set her mind to. She was a strong woman, no one ever saw her complain, she lived to make others happy, and that is how each and every one of us should live."

A strong pain of guilt shot up into Abigail's heart. At that moment she repeated to herself, "I have to be strong, I must be strong."

With her head down and her hands covering her face, Abigail felt a volcano of emotions wanting to erupt inside of her. Feelings of guilt, sadness, selfishness and anger, but with a deep sigh, she suppressed them. Again and again she repeated to herself, "I have to be strong, I must be strong." From behind her, Abigail felt someone place a compassionate, loving, caring hand on her shoulder. Her body melted as warm butter to a knife. That touch could not have come at a more opportune moment. Vulnerable and with an open wound, Abigail needed someone to acknowledge her pain.

Amongst the hospital's elite society, was the dashing CEO, Dr. Jacob Alvarez. His gaze landed on Abigail shrinking in her seat with her hands covering her face. Like a predator sneaking up to its prey, he began to prepare a scheme to win her over. His first move, hand on shoulder. Second move, tender, concerned look. Third move, ask her to dinner. A plan that never fails at a time like this.

Abigail turned around in her seat, noticing it was Dr. Alvarez's hand resting on her shoulder, she turned fifty shades of red. She tried to say something, but nothing came out. When she finally managed to get a word out, she couldn't stop talking. Nervous and stuttering she asked, "How are you, good morning, I'm sorry for your loss, how did you know Dr. Lourdes?" all of which had obvious answers, except for good morning, because it was evening. Completely flustered, Abigail stood to greet him with a handshake or a hug or a handshake or a hug or both. She noticed how amused Dr. Alvarez looked with her awkwardness. This made her feel worse; she wanted to crawl under a rock and hide. She had a terrible crush on him since med school; he was one of her professors. She never worked up enough courage to talk to him. Now there he was, standing behind her, with his hand on her shoulder, and she was turning into an imbecile right before his eyes.

Dr. Alvarez enjoyed having this effect on people, it made him feel important. He normally would not target a woman like Abigail; she appeared to be too wholesome and naïve for his taste. However, because he was getting older, he'd give her a trial run as "marriage" material. Dr. Alvarez asked to walk Abigail back to her car under his umbrella.

She felt so intimidated by him that she could hardly stand up straight; surely she shouldn't push her luck trying to walk next to him. As only a true gentleman would do, he offered her his arm for her to hold on to. Although tempted, she refused gracefully and pulled out her own umbrella. She didn't want to embarrass herself any further.

Abigail waddled through the puddles with her heels sinking into the mud; she could hardly walk. She sensed Dr. Alvarez's eyes on her as he walked directly behind her. Unexpectedly, an upsurge of wind lifted her dress and threatened to snatch her umbrella. She held on to the umbrella with her right hand as if it were her most valuable possession. With her other hand she did a Marilyn Monroe tuck to her dress. But her hat went flying off into the air. Relieved to feel the wind subside, she looked out of the corner of her eye, wanting to know if Dr. Alvarez was still walking behind her.

He was, and just to let her know he saw the entire ordeal, he said "Whew, that was close!" while holding her hat in his hand.

She didn't respond, she just wanted the ground to open and swallow her alive. The equivalent of a half block walk felt like a 5K marathon, she was struggling to get to the finish line. Everyone around her seemed to be walking just fine; it was personal what was happening between her and the storm. Twenty steps away from her car, the upsurge of wind reappeared, but this time with a vengeance. It flipped her umbrella inside out forcing the wires out of their sockets. The wires tangled through and around Abigail's hair, pulling so forcefully it felt as if she was going to fly away, which made it impossible for her to let go. Her dress was blown over her face leaving her completely exposed and blind. She couldn't see where she was going with her dress covering her face, but her hands were too busy trying to keep the umbrella from pulling all of her hair out and leaving her bald. Running to her rescue was Dr. Alvarez. As he struggled to untangle her hair from the wires, they both got soaked and nearly killed by lighting; luckily it hit a nearby tree instead. In her mind, all Abigail could say was, *strike me lighting, please strike me and put me out of my misery.*

In the few months following Dr. Lourdes's passing, Dr. Jacob Alvarez discreetly pursued Abigail. He made sure his work shift would coincide with hers. Abigail found it strange how often she was seeing him around. She could not imagine for one second that he was interested in her. After her exorcist, demon umbrella experience, she was too embarrassed to even look at him, much less speak to him. She still had a bald spot from that day.

One evening, as Abigail was trying to revive an eight-year-old boy, Dr. Alvarez showed up in response to a code blue. Just when Abigail thought she had lost the boy, Dr. Alvarez saved the day. At that moment, Abigail saw him in a different light. He looked exhausted from pumping the boy's chest; he didn't give up until the boy's heart was beating again. She was in love; *this man was a god.* They both walked out of the patient's room with a smile, sharing a sense of accomplishment that only doctors could feel when a life is saved. Abigail thanked him for showing up and not giving up. She asked him if he would allow her to buy him lunch as a thank you.

He accepted. *That was easy.*

The birds were singing louder than usual, the sun seemed brighter, and the air sweeter. Abigail woke up in a great mood; it was the day after she'd had lunch with Dr. Alvarez. She felt as if she was walking on soft, fluffy clouds. The first thing on her mind was Dr. Alvarez — or as he asked her to call him, "JACOB."

Oh my god, nobody called him Jacob!!!!

She was beyond excited. She wondered if she was ready to open her heart for love once again. She was terrified, after being hurt so many times; she'd have to take it slow. She remembered the day after Lourdes's burial, how she had determined herself to move on, to leave her past behind and live life as if her past didn't exist. That not only included the mystery of her adoption, but also her past failed relationships. Today seemed like a good day to make good on those promises she made to herself that day.

In the months and years that followed; slowly but surely Jacob became Abigail's life. She wanted to make sure she was the perfect girlfriend. After all, she realized how lucky she was that he had chosen her. All the women she knew wanted him, but who wouldn't? He was perfect: handsome, intelligent, intriguing, charming, and with impeccable taste. She took her role very seriously. She started to dress the way he wanted her to, maintained her weight at his recommended number, and last but not least, she alienated herself from everyone who didn't understand their relationship.

Yes, he had a wondering eye, but it was difficult for him not to; women practically threw themselves at him.

Yes, he had a bit of a temper, but that was not his fault. Not only was his job stressful, but she herself could be a handful. She couldn't be bothered with people who didn't "get" them, not even her father. She made many changes during the years following Lourdes's passing. The most important of them all was finding true love against all odds.

CHAPTER 5

Not Worthy of Him

It was a beautiful day, clear blue skies, not a cloud in sight. Driving with the Bentley's top down, breathing in the ocean air while admiring the heights of the mountains; was exactly what a perfect day was meant to be. Hair blowing in the breeze, Adele's "Rolling in the deep" blasting from the car speakers, and the warm sun shining bright on her face. Abigail was on her way to her beach house to meet with her love for their yearly much-needed vacation. Every year they took a month off from their busy careers to lay low there. They had been doing this since they started dating three years ago.

This was her first house. Her parents thought it was crazy to buy a beach house while living in a rental house. She, on the other hand, thought her month off would be something she would be looking forward to all year, so she wanted to make sure the location was the perfect place for her to escape. Her rental house was more like a dorm room, a place she came to sleep, eat, and go back to work. It made sense to her, anyway.

Her life was all about work, business meetings, consultations, conferences and teaching classes at the university once a week. Sometimes she wished she could have more time off, but for what, to do what? The only thing she wanted was to have a family, and that had not happened. So why waste time doing things she wasn't interested in? She wanted to be a wife and a mother more than anything in the world. Sometimes she wondered if it would ever truly happen.

She arrived at her safe haven, her beach house. What a feeling, she loved it there. She fell in love with the house as soon as she saw it. It was the only one she looked at while shopping for a house. It sat high on stilts above the sand with a dock attached to the back deck. She had it painted sky blue, with stark white trim, and professionally decorated to bring the ocean feel inside. Everything inside was white and ocean blue. The furniture had been custom designed for each room. The family room had ceiling to floor windows overlooking the ocean. A modern fireplace was installed directly in the center of the room, to provide a "water & fire" ambiance in the space. A leather white fluffy sectional sofa, accented with pillows of all shades of blues, was placed facing the windows. The open kitchen had an intimate feel. The countertops were made of earth toned granite. A long squared Island with six tall bar stools divided the kitchen from the living room. The cabinets were an antique white making the kitchen look cozy and inviting. She had wood floors installed to add warmth to the space.

Her favorite place in the house was what she called her sanctuary. She hired someone to build her a wooden cabana at the end of her dock. She wanted to be able to sit and literally touch the ocean with her feet. Nothing made her feel more vibrant than nature. If she could have it her way, she would either live in the midst of the forest with rivers and waterfalls all around her, or in a tent on the beach. Everything "nature" made her feel alive.

Fresh flowers were on the kitchen table; long-stem yellow roses in a tall glass vase, with a note attached. All the windows were open, making the white sheer curtains dance with the wind. Jazz was playing in the background. Scented candles were lit all around the living room, giving an ocean breeze fragrance that made her heart smile. She picked up the note attached to the flowers. It read, "Welcome back, we hope you find everything to your liking," signed: Chef Alfred & his crew.

The house was perfectly prepared to her taste. She looked around, peeked in the three bedrooms and then walked out to her cabana. This was her ritual every year. She made sure she arrived at the house first so that she could have some alone time to reflect. She kicked off her shoes and sat on the dock. With her feet in the water, she took a deep breath of ocean air and let out all of the negativity that she had allowed in. Then she reached under one of the floor planks to a secret waterproof drawer she had the builders install for her. She looked around to make sure no one was watching, then opened the drawer and pulled out something that held the mystery to her birth; her hospital birth nametag that simply read: Abigail and her date of birth.

Thoughts of Jacob filled her mind. He was dashing, handsome and sophisticated. His height alone made him instantly intimidating when he walked into a room. He stood at 6'2" with dark brown wavy hair. While his manly physique made him look strong and unreachable, his hazel eyes and thick eyebrows made him look loving and tender. There wasn't a woman on the planet that could resist Dr. Alvarez. The moment Abigail laid eyes on him, she fell in love. She admired him greatly. While he was giving his lectures, Abigail would daydream about a lavish wedding in which he would be at the end of the aisle waiting for her. She was surprised she passed his class with honors because she never listened to a word he said. She never pursued him though; she didn't feel worthy of him. At times, she swore she would catch him staring at her, although he denied it to this day.

The dinner table was perfectly set; Abigail's favorite personal chef always came through. She paid him a great deal of money to reserve him strictly for herself the entire month she was on vacation. Chef Alfred was a man in demand, but he seemed to genuinely like her. He made sure never to schedule anything else around that time. He didn't seem to care for Jacob much, though. She noticed Alfred tried to avoid him at all costs. It was kind of funny, almost like watching oil and vinegar when they were in the same room.

Chef Alfred had a magical touch; he created art with his food. He also always brought along a crew to create the perfect ambiance with décor. This year's first day dinner theme was, "The enchanting sea." Talk about a fairy tale. Dinner was set up at the cabana, with a round table for two placed in the center. The entire ceiling of the cabana was lighted with tiny hanging crystal like lights. The table was covered with a silky fabric that resembled melting gold. There was an oval crystal vase in the center of the table filled with floating candles of all shapes and sizes; it gave an impression of an above water chandelier, simply magical. The crew outdid themselves every time. As she complimented and thanked Alfred and his staff, she could see Alfred giving her "the look." She knew exactly what he was thinking.

She laughed and said, "Not this time, Alfred," but he did not look convinced.

Looking at herself in the mirror, Abigail could not imagine what Jacob saw in her. Sure, many men were attracted to her, but "Dr. Jacob Alvarez?" He was way out of her league. Every time she looked in the mirror, ever since she was a little girl, she had the same thought, "Who do I look like?" Her adoptive father was a dark skin man with jet black hair, his wife a redhead with freckles, both of them from Puerto Rico. Abigail was taller than both of them at 5'11." Her hair was brown with soft curls, her eyes brown and her skin olive. Her parents often received awkward stares from strangers. One time a person at the grocery store went so far as to ask them if her adoptive mom was her nanny. That really upset her mother; she would get very angry. Abigail felt as if it was her fault.

She said softly to herself, "I wanted so badly to look like my adoptive mom, maybe that way I could make her love me." While her father was working, her adoptive mother would mistreat her. She'd make her clean her sibling's rooms, do yard work and even wash everyone's clothes. Abigail felt as if she needed to do more to earn her love. One time when Abigail was seven years old she dotted her face with red marker to pretend they were freckles. When she showed her mom, she thought she was making fun of her and grounded her for a week. Abigail felt her eyes swell up with tears as she thought, *I could never do anything right in her eyes. Yet my father loved me unconditionally. It didn't matter if I had one arm and no legs or looked like a monster. I felt his acceptance and love every day of my life.*

She took one last glance in the mirror. Jacob should be there in an hour. She wore an elegant gold, satin, off-the-shoulder flowing dress, to match the theme of the night. Her hair was down past her shoulders, with soft, big curls. She wore the diamond earrings Jacob had given her for her birthday two years ago. She stepped out of her bedroom and walked towards the sliding door that led to the back porch.

***Chef Alfred took one look at her as she walked out onto the porch. The moon was shining on her beautiful, big brown eyes. She looked elegant, delicate, enchanting, mesmerizing, just like a fairy tale princess. As the breeze caressed her hair, it carried with it the sweet scent of her perfume. He took a few steps, gently grabbed her hand and walked her towards the table. He always waited for her approval of the setting before he left the premises; with the utmost respect and admiration, Alfred awaited her response.

"Well done Alfred, once again you have outdone yourself. Thank you."

Chef Alfred kissed her hand and started the music as he made his exit. Once again he gave her "the look." She laughed and waved him off.

Three hours later, there she was, sitting on the dock with her shoes off and feet in the water. Jacob never came. In the past, Jacob had told her not to contact him more than once if he didn't answer the first time, but she still tried contacting him several times; he didn't respond. She'd hope this time he wouldn't disappoint her, even though he had missed many of their dinner dates before. Abigail was desperately trying to believe that he loved her the way she loved him. She looked at the gourmet food, it was cold and inedible; the candles had all burned down and extinguished themselves in the water. The breeze off the water turned from refreshing to chilly. She let out a sigh and said "This time he didn't even call." Alfred was right when he gave her "the look," he knew he would do it again, as he had so many times before. Within minutes of Abigail coming to terms with the fact that Jacob might not show up for dinner, her phone rang. She ran to pick it up. *That should be Jacob*. She was sure he would have a good reason for not coming.

Out of breath, she answered, "Jacob?"

"No, sorry, it's Chef Alfred," said the voice on the other side.

Abigail went silent; she couldn't imagine why he would be calling at this time of night.

***Feeling awkward, Chef Alfred tried to think of what to say. He asked if he had left his iPad on the kitchen counter. Abigail began to sob, her tears coming from deep down inside her soul. She could not stop weeping. Her words wouldn't come out. Chef Alfred, hearing the pain in her voice, asked if she needed company.

How did he know Jacob had not shown up? That upset her, but she was too broken to argue. She answered, "Yes, Alfred that would be nice."

Within two minutes, her doorbell rang. Abigail was startled. She knew Alfred lived at least a thirty-minute drive from her house. *Who could be at the door, maybe Jacob?* She tried to compose herself as she opened the door. There, still wearing his white apron stood Alfred. She threw herself in his arms, completely surrendering to her pain. Through her tears she asked, "How did you get here so fast?" to which he responded, "I never left."

CHAPTER 6

Just Allow Yourself to Feel

Jacob woke up with the brightness of the sun shining through his bedroom window. He was so drunk the night before that he woke up with an unbearable headache. He felt as if he had forgotten something. Pouring himself a cup of coffee, he looked through his phone to jog his memory. He saw a few missed calls and texts from Abigail, he had lost count of the times he had told her that if he didn't answer the first time, then he must be busy. No need to call or text more than once.

He opened her text that read, "Hello sweetie, I hope I'm not disturbing you. I just wondered what time you would be arriving at the beach house, I thought we had agreed to have dinner together or maybe I just misunderstood. I love you."

That was when he realized what he had forgotten. With a slight grin, he said to himself, "Oh good, I thought it was something important, I'll call her later."

The aroma of freshly ground coffee and of the sweet cinnamon coming from Alfred's homemade Crème Brulee French toast filled the house. This was one of the things Abigail looked forward to eating every year. The most soothing, calming breeze was making its way through the open windows. The sound of the waves crashing against the shore was like a melody to her soul. She had fallen asleep on the couch while watching movies all night with Alfred. He tried his best to cheer her up by making gourmet popcorn and downloading as many comedies as he could find on Netflix.

Her makeup was undone, and her hair was in complete disarray. Although she felt ashamed to be seen that way; she could not stop laughing. Abigail opened her eyes to see Alfred in the kitchen cooking away, while dancing to 80s tunes. She started spontaneously, genuinely laughing, something she had not done in years. Poor Alfred could not dance to save his life.

*** *She never looked so beautiful to me than now,* Chef Alfred thought. Mascara marks down her face, her hair a perfect mess, pure simplicity, sincere perfection; she was the most stunning woman he had ever seen. It made him crazy that she didn't know it; she didn't believe it. The years he'd been working for her, he had seen her self-esteem get trampled on by Dr. Alvarez. But to him, just when he thought she couldn't be more beautiful, she was. He saw her laughing uncontrollably making fun of his dancing; he thought it was adorable how she laughed like a hyena. He had never seen this side of Miss Abigail; he was pleasantly surprised. It didn't matter that the source of her laughter was his terrible dancing; he liked seeing her laugh. As soon as he composed himself, he made the finishing touches on her breakfast table. It was set up on the deck overlooking the water... It looked delicate and elegant, the only thing he added were fresh flowers in a glass vase for a hint of color. Not much was needed in this setting, it was magical all on its own. The sun was shining softly on the ocean water reflecting delicate rays onto the deck; simply extraordinary just like her. He stood by the table waiting for Miss Abigail to give her approval so he could leave. She made her way to the deck, took one look at the setting and smiled. With a sweet, tender, but lonely look on her face, she asked Chef Alfred if he could stay and join her. He did.

Abigail excused herself to freshen up a bit. She took a quick shower and threw on a white sundress. Chef Alfred was relieved that he had a few extra uniforms in the guest room's closet in case of any accidents in the kitchen. While Abigail freshened up, he went into the guest room, showered and changed into a fresh white chef jacket and black trousers.

*** She was grateful Chef Alfred accepted her invitation to join her for breakfast. She didn't think she could bear to be alone. Her soul was wounded and her heart was shattered.For some reason, this time it hurt more than the other times.

Chef Alfred was sitting at the table waiting for her. When he saw her, he stood up like a gentleman and pulled the chair for her to sit. As she grabbed her coffee mug, she noticed he was quiet, pensive, and staring out into the ocean. She asked what he was thinking.

He didn't want to be disrespectful, therefore he told her it wasn't important, but she insisted. Reluctantly Alfred responded, "I'm wondering what hurt you so deeply throughout your life that made you feel unworthy of love and respect."

Abigail had never been asked that question before, no one had ever seen through her in that way. She looked away, her eyes swelled up with tears. She knew he was right. As if opening a faucet that had been closed for years, but so full with water that it was bursting to gush out, she began speaking.

"I don't know who I am, where I came from, who my parents are, why they gave me away, what was so horrible about me that they couldn't stand the sight of me and gave me away. I want to know what was so unlovable about me that not even my parents could love me."

She wept like a lost child, her tears cascading down her face without ceasing, her entire body shaking from a pain she had never allowed herself to feel. She stood and slowly walked to the railing. She yelled with all of her might out to the ocean, "MOM, WHERE ARE YOU? I WANT TO FIND YOU.

WHY DIDN'T YOU LOVE ME? I NEEDED YOU MORE THAN YOU CAN IMAGINE. PLEASE LOVE ME, PLEASE LOVE ME. MOM, PLEASE LOVE ME!!!!"

Abigail dropped to the deck floor in a fetal position; her entire body felt the weight of her pain. Chef Alfred kept his head down in reverence; he didn't want to interrupt her in any way. He was there for her and that was all that mattered. Abigail continued to talk. She told him that she felt there was a mystery behind her birth. How no one ever talked about how she had come to be adopted. How her only hope of knowing the truth was Dr. Lourdes, the woman who had named her, but she passed away in her arms before she could ask her. How she had spent thousands of dollars trying to find her birth parents and her birth information, but she would always arrive at a dead end. She recounted how much she had suffered at the hands of her adoptive mother, Mara. Speaking as if she was a child, Abigail told Alfred about her.

"She was cruel, yet I was always trying to win her over. I was at the top of my class, I kept my room clean, helped her around the house, did all I could for her to like me, but nothing worked, I was never enough. I never felt love or acceptance from her, only rejection."

The one time she gained enough courage to ask her father about her adoption, he told her that it didn't matter, that he loved her and would never leave her. With pain in her voice Abigail said, "my adopted mother overheard that conversation from the next room and yelled in an amused tone, 'Ask the garbage man.' I don't know what she meant. I guess she was making a joke of some sort, but it hurt. My father was furious. He went to her and said something in her ear, I'm not sure what he told her, but she was the nicest she had ever been to me that day."

CHAPTER 7

The Prince Turns Into A Frog

*J*acob packed a bag and decided to head out to the beach house. He wondered why Abigail hadn't answered his calls or texts. That bothered him because she always answered right away. If it wasn't because she was nice arm candy for his events, he wouldn't have lasted three years with her. She was a needy, insecure woman. Not to mention she didn't let him sleep with her stupid nightmares. Last year he had to sleep in one of the guest rooms because she practically cried all night after one of her episodes. "Get over it" was what he told her. Why couldn't she just look pretty and be quiet? He hated the drama.

Abigail was always buying Jacob things, helping him with his paperwork, doing his groceries, and picking up his laundry. She even asked him what she should wear or how to wear her hair. She portrayed herself as a confident woman, but she was far from it. He tried to break up with her several times, but she always begged and cried. Then she promised to do more, be better, look better, and he ended up falling for it and giving her another chance. He shouldn't have to put up with this, there were at least fifty women who would kill to be with him, and that was at work alone.

Jacob arrived at the beach house. He turned the key, opened the door, and found Abigail in the arms of Chef Alfred.

Chef Alfred was holding Abigail up; she had her arm around his neck as he helped her walk inside the house. She felt as if her legs were going to give way. Her body ached, her head pounded, her stomach was in knots. She had never allowed herself to experience such excruciating emotional pain.

Jacob walked in the door just as Alfred was helping Abigail inside. He looked furious, "you can't be serious Abigail, are you sick?" he said annoyed. "Why didn't you pick up the phone when I called? If you would've told me you were sick, I would have never come. What a waste of my vacation time." He then turned, looked at Alfred and said "are you making lunch? I'm starving!"

It took all of Alfred's energy not to punch him in the face. He needed to remain calm. It was Abigail's choice to make, not his. Abigail was the one that had to get to the point of valuing herself enough to not put up with Jacob. No saving her would keep her from falling into the same abusive cycle for the rest of her life; she had to break it on her own.

Abigail tried to compose herself. She told Jacob that she was fine. She then asked Chef Alfred if he could please start lunch. Jacob took off his shoes and flopped himself on the couch to watch TV, as if nothing happened. Abigail sat next to him and asked him about his day and tried to make small talk. As he always did, he ignored her.

Alfred proceeded to make lunch. Chopping the onion, he pictured Jacob's fingers instead. He asked himself time and time again, "What does she see in this man? Why can't she see how he uses her?"

Right then he heard Jacob tell Abigail to get off the couch that he didn't want to get sick with whatever she had. At that moment, Alfred picked up a cucumber and tried to hold himself back, but couldn't. With all his might he threw the cucumber and hit Jacob in the back of the head, then followed with the tomatoes, then the lettuce. He made the entire salad on top of Jacob's head. Laughing to himself, Alfred shook off that thought. He had to admit, it felt good to picture it.

Sal Lopez awoke in the middle of the night with a strange feeling; his heart was racing. He couldn't remember the last time he'd slept through the night without waking up this way. It had been almost three years since he last saw his daughter Abigail. He missed her terribly. The night she was born, as she arrived at the hospital, he was the first nurse she had been handed to after she was taken out of the dumpster. Sal would never forget that day. She was dirty and bleeding from her wounds. He loved her immediately. She looked up at him with those big brown eyes and he knew that he would be the one chosen to protect and love her. As he handed her over to Dr. Lourdes, he could tell she too saw something special in Abigail. So much so, that she surprised the entire staff by giving her the name Abigail. It saddened him that he couldn't tell Dr. Lourdes about the adoption. He knew she would frown upon the idea that her head nurse did not only become attached to a patient, but that he went as far as to adopt them. She would see it as unprofessional; he didn't want to take the risk of losing his job.

He missed the days when he took long walks on the beach with Abigail. They chatted about everything under the sun, he enjoyed talking to her. She had grown very close to him, more so than to his wife Mara. For some odd reason they didn't seem to get along so well. He thought surprising his wife with an adopted daughter would thrill her; since she had been abandoned as a child herself. He was wrong, Mara became indifferent and distant after he brought Abigail home. He couldn't understand it, Abigail was the perfect child; she had a contagious sense of wonder.

He liked to cook for her; she loved food almost as much as he did. He loved her so much. He spent an enormous amount of money to have all of her records destroyed, and would've paid more. He never wanted Abigail to look back and think her beginnings defined who she truly was. In his eyes, she was perfect.

Chef Alfred and his crew set up dinner and were dismissed for the night. All except one server stayed to serve the meal and clean up. Before they left, Abigail was called for her final approval of the setting. She looked forward to seeing their creation. It was always something different and magnificent. The strangest thing about it was that it was always what she was in the mood for, the setting as well as the menu. How in the world did they get it perfectly right every single time? Not once in the last five years had she been disappointed. Tonight was no different. They arranged a simple but elegant table for two on the deck. It was perfectly positioned for the most captivating view of the sunset. She smiled when she read the menu card. How did Chef Alfred know that she would be craving comfort food tonight? Food like the kind her father made. Answering her own question, she thought, *because she paid him the big buck, that's how*.

Her father made the most heartwarming typical Puerto Rican dishes in the world. She had grown up eating his food. People looked at her strangely when they saw her eating alcapurrias (beef patties made with green bananas). Tonight, Chef Alfred made a sampler appetizer plate with miniature Puerto Rican goodies. Empanadas, bacalaitos (codfish patties), sorullitos (corn rolls), alcapurrias (green banana patties stuffed with ground beef) and rellenos de papa (potato balls stuffed with ground beef). This was

61

followed by an avocado citrus salad and the entrée; Mofongo relleno de mariscos (fried and mashed green plantains filled with seafood). For dessert, nothing less than her favorite Flan de queso (cheese flan) served with a cafecito con leche hervida (Latte). She was in heaven. She only allowed herself this meal once a year to keep her weight from fluctuating, so she savored every bite.

As Jacob and Abigail ate, her gaze drifted towards the sunset. Abigail could not believe everything that came out of her that day. She had never broken down in front of anyone, much less an employee. Yes, Chef Alfred was a nice person and he made her feel safe and comfortable, but she could not help but wonder if she was paying him for that "niceness." She wondered if he felt as though he had to pretend to care because she was paying him a lot of money to do so. Whatever the case might be, there was no denying she felt different, lighter, almost as if some weight had been lifted from her.

Her mind was clearer, her spirit uplifted, and the turmoil inside of her had diminished. Her thoughts were rudely interrupted by the sound of Jacob sarcastically telling her to ring the bell so the server would bring dessert. When she looked down to find the bell, it was next to his hand. At that moment she felt anger rising. For the first time since she had been with Jacob, she caught a glimpsed of his ego. She responded in the same sarcastic tone "why don't you ring the bell? It's practically under your finger."

He looked up in disbelief; his eyes opened wide with fury. He grabbed the bell and threw it on her lap.

"Because I told you to do so." Jacob responded.

Abigail lifted her head, when she looked into his eyes, she knew she felt differently.

She wondered what she had seen in him. He was nothing but a pompous, self-absorbed, narcissistic, mean human being. He used people for his benefit, and when he was done, he got rid of them and left them lifeless. Like a movie, she could see the last three years flash before her eyes, all the belittling, the humiliations, the unfaithfulness, the lies, the control, the manipulation and the abuse. However, the most painful of all, was how she had allowed him to separate her from her father.

Jacob was so angry, he didn't finish his dessert. The hate in the eyes of Abigail was not something he was used to seeing in any woman. He was only used to seeing desire, admiration, and respect from everyone who knew him. He had to fix this situation and fast. He would teach her a lesson she wouldn't soon forget. He was Dr. Jacob Alvarez, and no one treated him that way.

Abigail slammed her bedroom door closed after giving Jacob a piece of her mind. She said things she had never said to anyone in her entire life. She replayed the conversation over and over in her head. "Do you really think you are that special Jacob? Who exactly do you think you are that you would ask me to ring a bell that is practically under your finger, GOD??? Well if that's the case, let me wake you up. You are far from being a god. No god would be so insecure that he would find his strength from belit-tling other people. No god would go around trying to prove his masculinity by sleeping with as many women as possible. You are no god sweetheart; you are nothing but a needy, narcissistic, pompous, over confident, power hungry, piece of horse manure. I'm just sorry it took me three years to see it." The more she thought about what she said, the more she thought, *what's wrong with me? Am I losing my mind?!!! If so, why am I enjoying it?*

By far, what surprised her most was when she grabbed the glass of red wine and spilled it on his Armani outfit, white shirt and khakis. It was like an out-of-body experience. She wanted to throw him over the railing, but figured he was too heavy to lift and she would only look stupid trying. Not to mention that it was the shore and the worst that could happen was that he'd get wet. Not enough reward for all of her trouble.

For some strange reason, even after having such a heated argument with Jacob, instead of crying her eyes out as she usually would when she made him unhappy, all she could think about was her conversation with Chef Alfred. Something happened to her after that, but she wasn't sure what it was.

It was the third day of Miss Abigail's vacation. After the intense two days she'd had, Chef Alfred wanted to make this breakfast extra special, even if she had to share it with Satan himself. Chef Alfred laughed out loud, he really hated that man. He would have his crew set up right on the sand by the shore. She needed some serenity, calmness and peace while watching the sunrise. Abigail loved nature, everything about it. As beautiful as she was, there was a simplicity to her that made her mesmerizing. He had seen her run to the beach early in the morning while the sun was still rising and get into the water in her pajamas. He loved the spontaneous side of her, those rare times that she allowed herself to be free. She only did these things when she thought no one was looking. Chef Alfred felt fortunate he had gotten a glimpse of some of those moments.

One of his favorite was when he saw her making a sand castle. Her brown hair glistened with the sun and danced in the wind. Her olive skin glowed. There was a sparkle in her eyes that could only be seen in a child. Her castle was probably the weirdest he had ever seen. It had four towers with rounded tops that looked more like spaceships, but it was beautiful to him because she made it.

The sun was barely rising as Dr. Jacob Alvarez woke up in the guest room. His night was a restless one. He had never been disrespected the way Abigail had done the night before. He banged Abigail's door open and stomped into her room without knocking.

She was sitting by the window staring out at the ocean. She had not slept at all. Her mind had drifted to the three years of hell she had lived with Jacob. She became angrier and angrier with every thought. How could she have allowed herself to lose sight of who she was and embraced who he said she was?

Abigail was startled when Jacob threw her bedroom door open.

Expecting an apology, Jacob looked at her with anger and asked "Do you have something to say to me Abigail?"

"Yes I do. Get out of my house Jacob!"

He began to laugh with the most sarcastic and evil laugh she had ever heard.

"You are kidding, right? Abigail, you know you can't do better than me. No one will ever put up with your drama and insecurities. You are nobody without me. It's because you know me that you have friends, respect and status. If I walk out that door, there will be no coming back. No begging and crying in the world is going to make me come back to you. You know that all the men you have had before me have left you. I've been the only one to put up with you. You will never be able to move on without me. You are not smart enough, pretty enough or confident enough to have a successful life without me."

Jacob was running out of things to say and Abigail didn't seem to be moved. He decided to move on to plan B. Speaking in a softer tone he said, "I was going to marry you; I planned to propose. You could kiss your dream of being married and having children goodbye." He hit below the belt by telling her that. He knew how badly she wanted that to happen.

Abigail felt herself crumbling and losing her strength. He enjoyed putting ideas of rejection into her mind to torture her and keep her under his control. When she was almost down, he went for the kill. He knew what would hurt her like a spear into her heart. He knew how badly she wanted to know who she was and where she had come from.

He continued, "Besides Abigail, what man would want to be married to you? You don't even know if you are an orphan, or worse you could be the daughter of drug addicts and murderers for all I know."

Cuddled in a fetal position with her head buried between her knees and arms around her legs, she braced herself. With the last ounce of strength she could muster she yelled, "GET OUT!!!!!"

Chef Alfred heard every word. He wanted to intervene, run to her rescue, but he knew he couldn't. It had to be her decision to make.

Jacob stormed to the guestroom to pack his things. His rage was taking over as thoughts ran across his mind. *What will I tell my colleagues? This will be the most shameful thing that has ever happened to me. To get dumped by someone like Abigail will go on record as pathetic. I cannot allow her to humiliate me like this. My reputation is at stake, even my career. People will lose respect for me.* He would not go down like this.

Abigail looked up from the floor; she had no tears left to shed. The only thing she wanted to do was hear her father's voice. She needed her father more than ever. She needed to be reminded of who she was. On her knees, she dragged herself across the floor and reached to get her cell phone but it was completely dead. She crawled towards the house phone. With her hands shaking, she picked up the receiver and dialed her father's number. Someone picked up immediately and Abigail yelled, "Daddy, I need you, Daddy!"

Jacob heard Abigail speaking on the phone; he immediately picked up the extension phone in the other room and began to eavesdrop.

On the other end Abigail heard a woman's voice say, "This is not your dad, this is his wife Mara. Abigail, what are you doing calling here? You are an ungrateful piece of garbage. After everything your dad has done for you, you stopped talking to him for years and expect him to respond? He hates you, Abigail. He never wants to see you again."

Abigail fell silent; she knew Mara was right. She didn't deserve him. She had betrayed him and he had every right to hate her.

After hearing Abigail's entire conversation with Mara, Jacob smiled and thought *this could not get any better*. As he was leaving the house he yelled, "I will make you pay for this Abigail. Your nightmare has just begun."

CHAPTER 8

Is This The End?

al Lopez's eyes filled up with tears when he thought about the last time him and his daughter Abigail were together. He made her favorite Puerto Rican meal. She was coming to introduce him to her boyfriend, Dr. Jacob Alvarez.

As soon as Jacob entered the house, Sal felt a weird vibe. The man seemed arrogant. Nonetheless, he shook it off. He liked to give people the benefit of the doubt. If anyone was able to see the good in people, it was him.

When Abigail made the introductions, she said, "Jacob, this is my dad, Sal Lopez," to which Jacob responded, "Don't you mean, 'Adoptive dad'?"

Sal could see his daughter getting flustered as she answered, "You know what I mean."

He came to her rescue and said to Jacob, "No, she means her dad," then hugged and kissed her on her forehead.

Abigail didn't seem to appreciate her dad's response; she looked terrified. Things only got worse as the evening progressed. From that day forward, he heard less and less from her until she stopped calling altogether. He longed to see his baby girl....

Two weeks had passed since Jacob left, and since Abigail had seen the light of day. She closed the windows and pulled down all of the blinds. She asked Chef Alfred to leave, but he refused. Every morning he came and opened her door slightly and slid her meals through a small crack. Abigail hated that he was pretending to care. This annoyed her; she wanted to be left alone with her pain. She told him that she would still pay him, but he still refused to leave.

She looked so fragile and tired; Alfred could not bear to see her that way. He tried the best he could to take care of her for the last two weeks. She didn't speak, didn't go outside and barely ate what he made her. He was glad to be there looking after her. He would carry her and feed her with his own hands, if that's what it took to heal her pain. She lost the sparkle in her eyes and with it the will to live.

By the second week, Alfred became worried. He wondered if he should try to call her father to talk some sense into her. But then he reminded himself that this was her journey and he should not intervene. Still, he could not help but want to rescue her. She didn't deserve this. He wanted to tell her how valuable she was, but deep inside he knew that she had to believe it for herself. Nothing he said or did would change that.

Abigail's bedroom door was locked; Alfred had not been able to slide her breakfast inside. It was close to eleven a.m. and Chef Alfred had not heard a sound come out of her room. He became desperate. He didn't know if knocking on her door would be too intrusive. He called her cell phone, but it went straight to voice mail. Either it was off or out of charge. So many things were going through his mind, he was overwhelmed with emotions. He had to see if she was okay. It didn't matter if it cost him his job. Taking a deep breath of bravery, he knocked on the door once, then twice, then three times. No answer. He proceeded to call her name softly.

"Miss Abigail, this is Chef Alfred, just checking up on you to make sure you are okay."

There was silence.

For the past week Sal had been feeling sadder than ever when he thought about his daughter. But today, he felt different. It was almost like a feeling of fear that she wasn't okay. The sleeplessness was worse than ever. Something was wrong, he could feel it. He prayed that she would be safe. Even though he had been giving Abigail time to come around, he always kept tabs on her with his friends at the hospital. He had retired, but he still kept in touch with all his friends there. They gave him a weekly report on his daughter and of her achievements as the great doctor she had become. He was the proudest father in the world to have a daughter like Abby. Not a day went by that he didn't miss her.

Sal sat on his back porch to look at pictures of Abby growing up. She had always been a daddy's girl. He could not shake the awful feeling he had today. He grabbed his phone to call her.

No answer. There was silence.

Chef Alfred took a step back and just when he was about to break Abigail's bedroom door open, she opened it. There she stood, looking more beautiful than he could ever remember. She wore a yellow sundress. All the window shades of her bedroom were open, and a gentle breeze was circulating around her room. The sun's rays were beaming through, reflecting on her delicate skin. Her hair was perfectly done, with long, soft, curls. He could not believe his eyes. She looked like a breath of fresh air.

Hiding his amazement, he asked, "Miss Abigail, what happened? I was worried because you didn't answer. I'm sorry to intrude but I was concerned about you; I'm glad you are fine. I will fix you lunch now."

"No Alfred I don't want you to fix me lunch. While I was in my darkest hour these past two weeks; I felt completely alone. I didn't want to live. I thought I had nothing to live for, but then I found this." She handed him an envelope.

He recognized the envelope and put his head down in shame. He knew he would be fired. "I'm sorry Miss Abigail; I'll get my things and leave."

Abigail gently took his hand in hers. "Don't go Alfred." He followed her to the terrace. She continued "You don't understand. I thought you were here pretending to care because I paid you, but when I opened the envelope and saw every single check I had given you for the past five years; I was in awe. I couldn't understand why you hadn't cashed them. It was then that I realized you really do care. All these years you have been here just because you care; I don't know why I had not seen it."

Alfred was at a loss for words, he never intended for her to find that money under these circumstances. He hid the envelope in her room with the intention that one day she'd find it and they would make a joke out of it. However, there was nothing he could do about it now; obviously fate had a better plan than he did. Alfred covered her hand with both of his and answered her question of why she had not seen it before by saying, "Because you weren't ready to see it Miss Abigail. Now was the time."

CHAPTER 9

Mission: Destroy

Mara would never forget her childhood. A woman and a man came to take her away. She held on to her mother's legs with all her strength and begged to be protected from those strangers. They were sent by the city's department of Children and Family to take her away from her alcoholic mother because of neglect. Her mother had a blank look to her that stayed tattooed in Mara's mind forever. She cried for days, months, even years. But then the day came when she stopped crying and never cried again. Not for her, not for anyone. Since then, she carried the shame and anger of it all. She was five years old at the time and lived in seven different foster homes after that day. She was never adopted, just thrown around like a piece of trash from garbage can to garbage can. She felt worthless, until the day she met Sal Lopez; he was the kindest man she had ever met. The more he learned about her, the more he seemed to love her. All the men before him abused and hurt her. Sal made her feel special and loved;

something she knew nothing about. He married her and they had three children. They were happy, until the day Sal brought Abigail home.

As soon as Mara saw her, she became angry and bitter. She thought, *why should she be adopted? What made Abigail so special? She had been found in a dumpster, for goodness' sake*. Mara didn't want her in her house and made sure she felt it every day of her life. After going down memory lane, she decided she would do it; she would go through with the plan.

Jacob sat outdoors in a small town bistro waiting for someone. He was anxious, looking around and running his fingers through his hair; he felt uneasy. He had not been himself since the "Abigail incident." This was a huge hit to his ego and it was killing him. He had to figure out a way to get her to come back to him begging on her hands and knees. He looked towards the entrance and there she was, standing at the doorway of the bistro; Mara, Abigail's adoptive mother. Jacob waived to her motioning with his hand for her to come to him. She sat down. There were no friendly exchanges of any sort. He was on a mission and there was no time to waste.

"Have you come up with anything?" he asked Mara.

"Yes I have" she said "and I'm sure this will bring her to her knees and back to you." She handed Jacob a box and told him, "This will destroy her."

There was so much Alfred wanted to share with Abigail; he had been waiting for this day for five years. The day he was interviewed for the job of becoming her personal chef, he brought his protégé with him, it was supposed to be his job. Chef Alfred was only there to oversee the interview and train him for the job. But the minute he set eyes on Abigail, he fell in love. There was a goodness, sweetness, and tenderness about her that was magnetic. From that day forward, he knew he wanted to remain close to her, even if it meant cooking for her one month a year. Alfred laughed when he thought about the reaction of his parents.

Alfred's parents were heirs to a throne. They lived in mansions all of their lives, as did all of their ancestors. But they were hopeless romantics at heart. They both laughed and thought Alfreds would be the most romantic love story ever told. He adored his parents. They had always supported him in everything he did, even if it didn't seem "prestigious" enough for other heirs to the throne. They taught him to live out of passion and principle, and to never compromise who he was on the inside to impress someone from the outside. Learning that lesson had surely paid off, because here he was, with the woman of his dreams by his side.

He had to pace himself as difficult as that would be; there was much healing to be done on her part. If it were up to him he would marry her right then. He could hardly wait to show her a life and a love she never thought possible.

Chef Alfred and Abigail talked for hours. It was as if they had been friends for years. They talked about their childhood, their dreams and their fears. Abigail laughed until she couldn't breathe when Alfred told her about why he accepted the "chef" job. She felt silly for thinking that he was there for the money. But she couldn't deny it felt special to think that a man like him had chosen to play that role just to be close to her.

After spending the entire day talking, sharing and laughing, they realized they had not eaten all day long; they were starving. She had not felt this hungry in weeks. Alfred offered to cook something up for them, but she refused. She wanted to take him out to dinner. Chef Alfred thought about a secluded small town where he vowed to only take someone he loved. It was colorful and lively. He found out about it because his parents received a tip that there was an Italian elderly chef there who had the secret to authentic Italian cuisine. Somehow his parents managed for him to cook under that chef for a year. This was worth more than gold to him. He learned so much more than cooking from that old man. He quickly suggested it to Abigail; she was thrilled, Italian cuisine was one of her favorites. He insisted they drive in his car. To Abigail's amazement Chef Alfred's "work" car was a cherry red BMW 650 convertible. She'd always pictured him driving a catering truck.

Alfred was on cloud nine. Every time he glanced over to the passenger's seat and saw Abigail sitting next to him, he was afraid he'd wake up and realize it was all a dream. He had thought about this moment for so long he could hardly believe it was real. He wanted to hold her hand, to touch her hair, hug her and tell her she would always be loved. But he had to pace himself, she was not ready.

Within thirty minutes they were driving into what Abigail thought to be the most joyful town she had ever seen. Every building was painted in vibrant colors; there were plants and flowers everywhere. As Alfred drove around town, she kept leaning out of the car to see more. She didn't know a place like this existed. She noticed Alfred staring at her and became flustered. She realized she must seem like a child to him, the way she was excitedly looking at the town. But he just laughed with a sparkle in his eyes that she had never seen in anyone. It did however, give her the same warm feeling that her father's look gave her; a feeling of love and acceptance. She didn't know what to make of it and she didn't feel a need to figure it out. For now, she would just enjoy.

As they walked the rustic brick paths of the historic town, she felt as if she was floating on a cloud. They arrived at "La Cucina," the restaurant he did his practice in. She remembered Alfred telling her that reservations to this restaurant had to be made a year in advance, yet they went directly inside. It gave her a warm feeling to know that Alfred was trying so hard to impress her. She could tell Alfred had informed someone about their arrival because the waiters were on the lookout. She wanted to laugh. It was so sweet of him to go out of his way like this for her. The staff was whispering, giggling, and giving him pats on the back as they walked in. Everyone seemed to love Chef Alfred. One of the men led them to a staircase. When they reached the top she stayed speechless. There was an impressive black iron gate entangled with vines that led to a cobblestone patio overlooking the ocean.

The food was exquisite. She was glad that Alfred loved food as much as she did, that way she didn't feel judged when ordering everything on the menu.

The night couldn't have been more enchanting. The conversation flowed; it felt natural, genuine, and real. Abigail was just waiting for someone to wake her up. There was no way feeling this free could be real. He didn't even seem to mind her hyena laugh that her "ex" hated so much.

Alfred was just as adventurous as she was. After dessert, he dared her to climb down a vine on the wall that led to the beach. No one could dare her to do anything because she loved a challenge. She immediately removed her shoes, tied her dress between her legs and down she went. Alfred followed after her laughing uncontrollably. She in turn dared him to get into the water with all of his clothes on. He agreed, but not without taking her with him. He chased her along the shore until he caught her. He picked her up and carried her into the water. The laughter could be heard from miles away. This was one of the happiest days of her life.

They drove back to the beach house, soaked, and drunk with laughter. As Alfred was walking Abigail to the door, they noticed a FedEx box was placed on the floor by the front door. It read, "To: Abigail Lopez," with no return name or address.

CHAPTER 10

The Calm Before The Storm

*J*acob was anxious. Two weeks had passed since he left the beach house and still no word from Abigail. She didn't answer his secretary's calls or her texts. He wondered if he even read them.

How selfish could she be? Thought Jacob, *Doesn't she know the impact this would have on my reputation?* His thoughts were interrupted by Zonde, his Greek goddess look-alike, personal secretary. He called on her when he was stressed, which was often. It thrilled him to use a woman as beautiful as her for his carnal satisfaction. It made him feel irresistible.

"Are you thinking about her?" Zonde asked.

Jacob hated to be questioned. "What do you care who I'm thinking about? Get dressed and go home. I'm done with you for today."

Humiliated, Zonde picked up her overnight bag and headed down the hall towards the elevator. He watched her walk away. She had one of the sexiest walks he'd ever seen in a woman, even when stomping away upset, she looked gorgeous. Her short blonde Marilyn Monroe hair was the first thing that attracted him about her. Mocking her, he yelled "same time tomorrow Zonde" he knew she'd come.

Why couldn't Abigail be more like Zonde quiet and obedient? He wondered if the plan he and Mara had come up with was going to work. If it would actually break Abigail enough to have her run back to him. He was not a patient man; this waiting was eating him up. She would pay for every minute of anxiety she had caused him.

Chef Alfred picked up the box. "Where do you want me to put it, Miss Abigail?"

"It's Abby to you, Chef Alfred."

"In that case, it's Alfred to you, Abby."

They smiled sweetly at one another.

Glancing at the box Abigail said, "It's probably medicine samples; I order some every year to donate to the free clinic here in town. That's strange; I don't remember ordering any this year. Just throw it anywhere. I'll go through it tomorrow."

As she stepped away towards the living room, Alfred took her hands in his. "Thank you for the most wonderful day I have ever had Abby. You are truly special." He gently kissed her hand and said goodnight.

Abigail's eyes began tearing up. *How could he say that? She had been herself. No pretending, no impressing, and no trying to use the perfect words. She had been simply Abby and that seemed to be enough.*

She had a good night's sleep for the first time in a long time. As the sun rose, she opened the doors to her bedroom terrace and invited the sun in. A lady server knocked on the door requesting permission to enter.

She was carrying a tray with breakfast on it. "Good morning Miss Abigail. I have orders from the chef not to allow you out until you eat everything on this tray." She said smiling.

Abigail burst into a joyous laugh. "Oh yeah, and how does the chef expect me to eat all of this food by myself? And why are there two coffee mugs on this tray?"

Abigail could see Alfred trying to hide behind the server, but there was no way he could. He was 6'1, with strong broad shoulders and she was a tiny 4'9, 90 lb woman. Alfred peeked out from behind the server like a mischievous little boy. His dreamy baby blue eyes were giving him away; he looked adorable. He responded, "It would be my pleasure to join you, if you're sure you don't usually drink out of two mugs." They both laughed. With a gentle, caring voice, Alfred asked, "Good morning, Abby. How did you sleep? How are you feeling today?"

She poured coffee for the both of them.

For the next two weeks Alfred and Abigail spent every waking moment together; he arrived early in the morning with something special planned for them to do. Abigail had never felt this cared for before by any man other than her father.

With every passing day, she missed her dad more and more. Alfred reminded her of him in so many ways. They both had an undeniable way of making her feel at ease and secure. She wanted to see her dad, even if he hated her. She had to hear him say it from his own lips. Jacob on the other hand, it surprised her that she had not missed or even thought about him for days.

One morning as the sun was rising, Abigail grabbed Alfred's hand. "Follow me, Alfred."

They walked outside towards the cabana. The morning dew was still on the leaves. The freshness of a new day could almost be touched. They sat on the edge of the dock. After reminiscing about their week together, Abby felt secure enough to open her secret drawer and show Alfred her nametag.

"This is the only thing I have from the day of my birth. I keep it because it gives me a lifeline to that day. I guess I'm hoping one day it would reveal all of the mystery."

Alfred, with soft tenderness, took the nametag from her hand and lovingly said, "Abby, regardless of what that mystery entails, it doesn't change who you are. You could have come from outer space, with alien parents and have ET as your brother, and you'd still be the most amazing woman I know. Your presence imparts joy. There is a simplicity about you that makes you more beautiful than any other woman on the planet. I love everything about you: your gentle spirit, your spontaneous impulses and yes, even your hyena laugh."

At that admission, she could not help but display the laugh right then.

Alfred continued, "What I'm trying to tell you is that even though I see it's important for you to know where you came from, I want you to remember that it cannot change who you have become."

It was the last day of her vacation. Alfred made her an unforgettable picnic lunch on the sand by the shore.

After lunch, as they walked towards the dock, Abigail remembered something. "Alfred, I just realized I leave tomorrow and I never delivered the box of medicine samples to the hospital."

She sat on the kitchen floor with a pair of scissors and opened the box. In utter shock, she said, "What in the world is this?"

CHAPTER 11

Dried Up Tears

*S*al Lopez could not wait another minute. His wife Mara told him that she ran into Jacob and that Abigail was fine. She said that Abby was on vacation at her beach house. Nonetheless, he still felt uneasy. He needed to hear her voice. He felt as if he had to see her, hold her. It was a strange feeling that he hadn't felt before. She was due back in town tomorrow, but he didn't know if he could wait another day. Something was going on with his baby girl and he needed to find her.

Sal got in his car and took on the three-hour drive to Abby's beach house.

Abigail looked inside the box; it was filled with old newspapers. She took the first one out and proceeded to read.

The Daily

Sunday, August 30, 1975

Dumpster Baby

A baby girl was found inside a dumpster near Metro Hospital. Sources say she was completely covered in trash, she had wounds caused by the debris. No one is sure if she will make it.

At first glance she wasn't sure what she was reading or what this could be about. She turned over the box to see if she had missed who it was from or perhaps to try and gather clues, but there was nothing. She read the newspaper again, this time with a knot in her throat. She wondered if this had been a patient of hers, but she knew she would surely remember something as tragic as a baby found in a dumpster.

Taking a closer look, she noticed the date on the newspaper; it was her very own date of birth. She became cold. Chills ran up and down her back, desperately she began to yell, "NO! Please God, NO!"

Chef Alfred was gathering the dishes from lunch when he heard Abigail scream. He dropped everything; the plates shattered on the floor as he ran towards her. As soon as he could tell she wasn't physically hurt, he sat by her side on the floor and put his arms around her. He waited until she was ready to share what it was that was hurting her so deeply. Without saying a word Abigail handed the first newspaper to Alfred. She thought that perhaps she was overreacting. Maybe her desperate quest to know where she came from was leading her to conclusions. It could all be a deranged coincidence; with Alfred by her side, she was able to read the second newspaper.

The Daily

Monday August 31, 1975

Dumpster Baby Adopted

The police is on the look out for the person that threw the baby girl in the garbage dumpster. A local male nurse by the name of "Sal Lopez" has adopted the dumpster baby. Sources say the baby was given the name ABIGAIL by hospital staff.

She whispered, "Please let this be a nightmare," but it wasn't. There was no denying that it was her. Sal Lopez was her adoptive father and she was the dumpster baby. Abigail put her hands on her head, entangling her fingers through her hair, she began to pull, desperately trying to feel a different pain than the one she was feeling inside. She wanted to hit herself, cut herself. Ending it all would be easier than living with that truth.

Chef Alfred didn't leave her side for one second. By then he knew what was happening and there was no way he was going to let her go through this by herself. Gently he grabbed her hands and stopped her from hurting herself. She wrapped her arms around his neck and clung to him tightly. No words were spoken between them.... Her pain was too great for tears. All he could hear coming out of her were moans of anguish. She took a deep breath, and gathered just enough courage to pick up the last newspaper.

Her worst fear had come true. Her parents never loved her. They had thrown her away without a second thought; they were drug addicts and now they were dead.

A plunging pain dashed across her chest. She felt nauseated, and with a force she couldn't control her trembling body forced her to vomit. Everything inside her wanted to convulse. Her body needed to let out the pain but she refused to let out a tear. Anger was what she wanted to feel. She stood up from the floor and began to hit the wall repeatedly with her fist until she bled. Only one thing came repeatedly out of her mouth.

"WHY DIDN'T I DIE? WHY DIDN'T I DIE?!"

Chef Alfred tried to stop her from hurting herself. He grabbed her by her waist and pulled her towards him. She tried to pull away by pushing him, but he held her closer. When she looked in his eyes, she saw tears. Alfred understood her pain.

Abigail broke free of Alfred's arms and ran out of the back door. He knew she needed to be alone. She ran across the shore, she ran and ran trying to get as far away from her truth as possible. She ran until she couldn't run anymore. Her legs grew weak, her body limb, surrendering to her pain she dropped to the sand. As if in a trance Abigail saw her life flash before her eyes. She couldn't comprehend why her father would choose her. She yelled as if she was speaking to her father.

"You could have chosen a perfect baby, but you chose me. You must have seen something special in me. Throughout my life you have been my counselor, my protector, my refuge and my rock. When I was sick, you were there. When I was sad, you held me. When I felt alone, you reassured me. You were all I've ever needed. Thank you Daddy... thank you.... thank you for changing the course of my life."

As Abigail began to see herself through her father's eyes, valuable and worthy of love, she slowly regained strength. The voice of Alfred lingered in her mind. "Abby, regardless of what that mystery entails, it doesn't change who you are."

Filled with hope Abigail rose to her feet and began to run back home. In the distance she could see someone running out of her beach house in her direction. As she got closer she recognized who it was...

With a trembling voice she yelled, "DADDY!!!!"

Abigail ran faster, there was an urgency in her step.

Sal saw Abigail running towards him and for a moment he envisioned her as his precious little girl.

Her daddy wrapped her in his arms and lifted her off her feet. Wiping the tears from the eyes; he twirled her around.

He kissed her forehead and held her tightly.

"Daddy, do you love me?"

"Yes baby girl, forever and always."